The Haunted Hotel

Contents

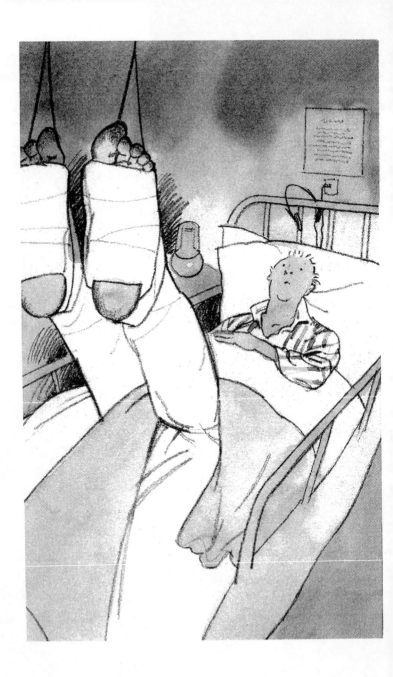

The Haunted Hotel

Brandon Robshaw

Published in association with
The Basic Skills Agency

Hodder & Stoughton

A MEMBER OF THE HODDER

Acknowledgements
Cover: Dave Smith
Illustrations: Mike Bell

Orders; please contact Bookpoint Ltd, 39 Milton Park, Abingdon, Oxon OX14
4TD. Telephone: (44) 01235 400414, Fax: (44) 01235 400454. Lines are open
from 9.00–6.00, Monday to Saturday, with a 24 hour message answering service.
Email address: orders@bookpoint.co.uk

British Library Cataloguing in Publication Data
A catalogue record for this title is available from the British Library

ISBN 0 340 77263 8

First published 2000
Impression number 10 9 8 7 6 5 4 3 2 1
Year   2005 2004 2003 2002 2001 2000

Copyright © 2000 Brandon Robshaw

Typeset by GreenGate Publishing Services, Tonbridge, Kent.
Printed in Great Britain for Hodder and Stoughton Educational, a division of
Hodder Headline Plc, 338 Euston Road, London NW1 3BH, by Atheneum
Press, Gateshead, Tyne & Wear

1

My Story

I'm lying in a hospital bed.
Both my legs are in plaster.
My spine is damaged, too.
If I'm lucky I'll be able
to walk again in a few months.

I won't walk like I used to.
I'll creep along, with a limp.
I used to play football.
I won't be doing that again.

Still, I don't complain.
I reckon I've had a lucky escape.
I escaped from the Haunted Hotel.

I still dream about it sometimes.
Then I wake up in a cold sweat.
It's a relief to find myself here in hospital.
But then I'm afraid to go back to sleep.
I wish those dreams would stop.

Maybe if I write it all down,
I'll get over it.
Get it out of my system.

This is what happened to me
in the Haunted Hotel.
You won't believe a word of it, of course.
Nobody will.
But it happened, all the same.

2

A Place to Stay

I didn't go looking for the Haunted Hotel.
I was just looking for a place to stay.
I'm a sales rep.
I go from town to town,
selling ladies' underwear to shops.

One night, I ended up
in a town I'd never been to before.
I didn't know any hotels.
It was getting late,
so I chose the first one I saw.
I still don't know what it was called.
It was a large, dark building
near the station.
A dim yellow sign said 'Hotel'.

I parked my car,
got my bag out of the boot
and went in.

The foyer was dimly lit,
with creaking floorboards.
There was no one about.

I went up to the desk.
It was covered in dust and cobwebs.
There was a bell,
so I rang it.

'Yes?' said a woman's voice.
Then I saw her.
An old, old woman
in a little back room behind the desk.
She was sitting in a rocking-chair,
knitting.
The room was covered in cobwebs.
As I looked at her,
I felt uneasy.
Her face was dirty too.

3

Room 13

'What is it?' asked the old woman.
Her voice creaked,
like the floorboards.

I stared at her dirty face.
Maybe I should have turned round
and left right then.
But it was late and I was tired.
I didn't see why I should run away,
just because an old woman had a dirty face.

'I'd like a room for the night,'
I said.
The old woman smiled,
showing a set of brown teeth.
'Frank!' she called out,
in her creaky voice.
'Frank!'

A porter came shuffling down the hall.
His face was dead white.
His head was completely bald.
His eyes were dark and deep-set.
He was as thin as a skeleton.
'Show the gentleman to Room 13,'
said the old woman.

Frank stared at me.
Then he picked up my bag
and shuffled away down the hall.
I followed.

We went up a dark, narrow
flight of stairs.
We came to a door
with 13 on it.
Frank let my bag fall to the floor.
He didn't move.
Perhaps he was waiting for a tip?
I gave him a pound.

'Thank you,' he said.
His voice was a whisper.
'Are you staying long?'

'Just the one night.'

Frank smiled.
'That's what you think,'
he whispered.

'Here's your room key.'
He turned and shuffled away
down the passage.
I couldn't be sure,
but I thought I heard him laughing
to himself.

I shrugged.
I unlocked the door of my room
and went in.

4

A Strange Smell
and
an Evil Portrait

There was a strange smell in the room.
A dark, heavy smell.
I didn't know what it was,
but I didn't like it.

I went to take a shower.
I felt nervous and jumpy.
I kept thinking I could hear a voice
above the noise of the shower.
It was very faint,
but it sounded like 'No! No!'
I switched the shower off and listened.
Nothing.

I dried myself and went back into the
bedroom.
I didn't like the room much.
There were dark heavy curtains,
the furniture was dark and heavy
and that dark, heavy smell still hung in the air.
On the wall was a picture
of a fat old man with thin lips,
bulging eyes and a pointed nose.
It was a nasty face –
like some evil old bird of prey.

Then I thought I heard the voice again.
It was louder this time.
'No! No! Get away from me!'

Then silence.
The dark, heavy smell seemed to grow
stronger.
And suddenly, I knew what it was.

It was blood.

5

Room Service

I didn't like this place one little bit.
It was giving me the creeps.
I rang the bell for room service.

An age went by.
Then the white-faced porter shuffled in.
'Yes sir?'

'I'd like another room, please,' I said.
'This one's got a horrible smell in it –
like blood.'

'Blood, sir?'

'Yes, blood!
Can't you smell it?'

The porter smiled.
'I expect I'm used to it.'

'Well, I don't want to get used to it.
I'd like another room.'

'All the other rooms are full, sir,'
whispered the porter.

I was sure this wasn't true.
But there wasn't much I could do.

I pointed at the picture on the wall.
'Take that thing away, anyway,' I said.
'I can't sleep with that
staring down at me.'

'I can't do that, sir.
He wouldn't like it.'

'Who wouldn't?'

'Mr Snell, sir.
The manager.
He's got a terrible temper.'

'So have I!' I said.
'Take it away
or I'll report you to Mr Snell in the morning!'

'I don't think you will, sir,' said the porter.
He laughed and moved towards the door.

'What sort of place is this?'
I asked angrily.
'Is everyone mad?'

'You'll get used to it, sir,'
whispered the porter.
'When you've been here a few years.'
The door closed behind him.

6

Mr Snell,
The Manager

I opened the window.
A cold breeze blew in
– but it was better than that sickly smell of
blood.

I turned the picture of Mr Snell
to face the wall.
Then I got into bed
and tried to sleep.

I tried to relax.
I tried counting sheep.
I tried lying in different positions.
But nothing worked.
I was too nervous to sleep.

I kept hearing noises.
Voices. Doors opening and closing.
Feet running up and down stairs.
Distant screams.
Then that voice shouting,
'No! No! Get away from me!'

I heard a clock strike twelve.
Then one.
Then two …

And then – bang!
A sudden loud noise from across the room.

I jumped out of bed,
trembling,
and switched the light on.

The picture on the wall had turned round.
Mr Snell was staring at me,
with a smile on his thin lips.

As I stood there,
frozen to the spot,
he stepped down out of the picture frame.

7

New Blood, Fresh Blood

He walked slowly towards me.
In his right hand,
he held a silver kitchen knife.
His left hand was twitching.

'I'm so glad you came to stay,' he said.
'We need some new blood here.'
He licked his lips.
'New blood,' he said. 'Fresh blood.'

'No! No! Get away from me!'
I screamed.

He smiled.
'It's a long time since I've heard that,'
he said.
'It's so good to hear it again.'

He was between me and the door.
There was no escape.
He looked me up and down.
He fingered the knife.
'I hardly know where to start,' he said.

And then I remembered.
I had left the window open.
I turned and dived through it.

As I fell,
I heard a howl of disappointment
from Mr Snell.
Then there was a great thud
and a sharp pain.
I blacked out.

8

The Ruin

When I awoke, it was dawn.
The sky was grey and
the ground was damp.
Birds were singing.

At first, I didn't know where I was.
Then it all came back to me.
I tried to get up and run.
But my legs wouldn't work.
I fell back to the ground.

I looked up at the Haunted Hotel.
Any minute now,
and Mr Snell would come out
with his kitchen knife ...

But nothing happened.
And then I noticed something strange.
The building was in ruins.
It might have been a hotel once,
but it wasn't any more.
The roof had fallen in.
The windows were boarded up.
Weeds poked through the cracks in the bricks.

I couldn't understand it.
I passed out again.

9

A Lucky Escape

Someone found me lying there
in the end.
They called an ambulance.
And the ambulance came and brought me
to this hospital.

So here I lie,
waiting for my legs to get better.
I've asked a few questions
about the place where I was found.
It turns out that
there was a hotel there once.
The last manager was called Mr Snell.
One night he went crazy
and killed all the guests and the staff
with a kitchen knife.
That was about fifty years ago.

I reckon I've had a lucky escape.